VOYAGE
TO THE
EDGE OF THE WORLD

Lesley Sims

Illustrated by Peter Wingham

Designed by Kim Blundell

Edited by
Rebecca Heddle

Series Editor: Gaby Waters

Contents

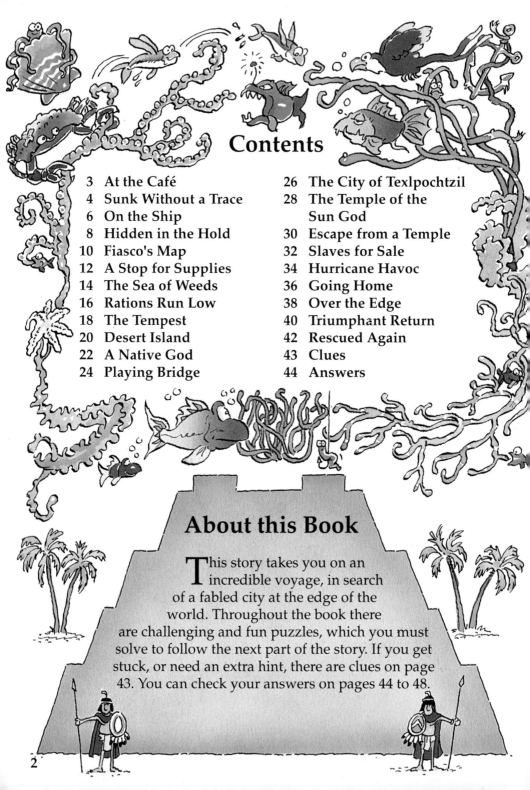

About this Book

This story takes you on an incredible voyage, in search of a fabled city at the edge of the world. Throughout the book there are challenging and fun puzzles, which you must solve to follow the next part of the story. If you get stuck, or need an extra hint, there are clues on page 43. You can check your answers on pages 44 to 48.

At the Café

It was the first day of Charlie and Will's stay in Parilla. They had just escaped a boring shopping trip with their parents. Now they sat at a café eating ice cream, and wondering what to do next.

Charlie read a tourist leaflet and groaned. Parilla wasn't the kind of seaside resort she'd imagined. "I suppose we could take out a rowing boat," she said.

Guide to Parilla

Welcome to Parilla where the past comes alive! Birthplace of the explorer Christofe Catastrofe (b. 1359), Parilla has many attractions.

Living History Ship - an imitation 15th-century galleon manned by actors, plus 47 museums, listed on pages 2-4.

Marine Exhibition - includes the Pink Parilla Pebblefish, only found in the waters near Parilla.

The Royal Palace - monument to Queen Isabella I. Free glass of Parillan Punch with every ticket.

Sick of sightseeing? Rent a deluxe boat from the fisherman on the jetty. All boats have a genuine certificate of seaworthiness.

Sunk Without a Trace

Will and Charlie left their ice cream and went to the jetty. But they could only see one old boat. Shopping might be safer, thought Charlie as she paid for it.

Will raced ahead. "Come on," he said. "Rowing's easy." Soon they were heading out into open sea.

"Easy, huh?" Charlie said. Will strained on the oars and steered straight into a rock.

"Bail out!" cried Charlie but Will was reaching for a bottle which was floating by.

Seconds later, they were splashing in the water as the boat began to sink.

"Are you crazy?" spluttered Charlie, as Will emerged holding the bottle triumphantly. "We're almost drowned and all you care about is an old bottle. HELP!"

But there was no one to hear her. The only thing in sight was a barrel encrusted with barnacles and seaweed. They clambered onto it as it bobbed past.

They floated in silence, hearing only the waves and the occasional cry of a gull. The sun warmed their wet skin. The barrel rocked them gently. Time seemed to stand still. . . until, as if from nowhere, an old-fashioned sailing ship appeared. Will and Charlie blinked in surprise and looked around. Suddenly, several things looked different. **Compare the two pictures. What looks different?**

On the Ship

Minutes later, Will and Charlie and the barrel were hauled aboard the ship. They stood dripping on its rough wooden deck, among a motley bunch of sailors. Huge white sails flapped above them and there was a musty, fishy smell. "Can you take us back to Parilla?" asked Will nervously.

"No chance!" said a bald man. "We're off to the edge of the world on a voyage of discovery." Will and Charlie looked puzzled. "We're under orders from Queen Isabella to stop for nothing in our quest for the Potion of Eternal Life."

Will and Charlie looked baffled. "Don't you know anything?" the man said. "This voyage is the talk of Parilla. We're tracing the route of Christofe Catastrofe, who set sail 100 years ago and didn't return." Will shook his head in confusion as the others joined in.

> We're all doomed if you ask me. We'll fall off the edge before we find anything.

> But I'm a seller not a sailor. . . bleugh!

> No one knew what became of Catastrofe. But now his charts have washed ashore in bottles.

> He found the city of Texlpochtzil at the edge of the world and a potion that lets you live forever!

> Try to be sick in the sea this time, Marco.

"Silence on deck!" shouted a voice from above. An imposing figure in a silly hat appeared on an upper deck glaring at the crew. "Is that salesman still being sick?"

Then his gaze fell on Charlie and Will. "Who are THEY?" he roared. "Am I, Fiasco da Balmia, the great explorer, running a ship for waifs and stray. . . HEY!" He gave a gasp of surprise and ran down to Will.

"Catastrofe's last bottle!" said Fiasco, snatching it. The wet bottle slipped from his fingers and smashed on the deck. A soggy roll of paper fell out. As Fiasco picked it up, the paper fell apart.

Can you fit the pieces together?

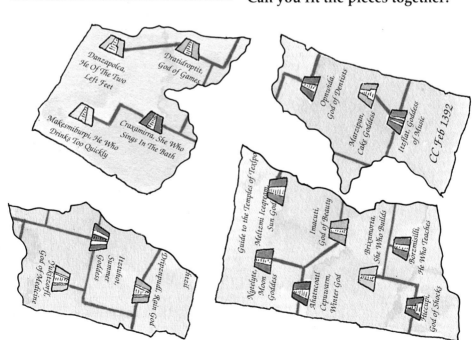

Hidden in the Hold

Fiasco held the pieces together. Will glanced at them over his shoulder, before Fiasco pocketed them and turned to the barrel. "Bob! Open this!" he called. The bald man swung a hatchet wildly at the barrel.

This is my record of the Azca people, who live at the edge of the world. The charm is a key which allows entry to their city and its temples.
C. Catastrofe 1392

The crew crowded around eagerly as Bob reached through the splintered lid. But the only things inside were a book and a small green charm on a leather string. Fiasco's eyes lit up. He grabbed the book and opened it.

"Catastrofe's diary!" exclaimed Fiasco. "I'll keep this." Then he pointed to a skinny boy, not much older than Will and Charlie. "Luiz! Take these two to the hold. They can wait there until I decide what to do with them."

Luiz led them down a ladder, into the depths of the ship. It was dark and dank, and grew stuffier and smellier the lower they went.

At the bottom, there was an overpowering stench of pickled fish, old onions and sweaty socks. Luiz thrust an oil lamp and some dry clothes at Will.

"This is the Living History Ship, isn't it?" said Charlie, thinking of the leaflet she'd read at the café. Luiz just shrugged and left.

"He's almost too good to be an actor," said Charlie. "In fact, all of them are." She pulled on a grubby, moth-eaten tunic. "This is all too realistic," she added. But Will wasn't listening. Something in a gloomy corner had caught his eye.

Half-hidden by a sack was a velvet bag, with a mirror poking out of it. The bag looked new and out of place in the dingy hold. Will emptied it and found a letter. It seemed to be in a foreign language - or was it?

What does the letter say?

O Geidy!

Levi ter cess ruo. Yleb alcit pyr, ceht rof kool seilp Puss ocsa if nit. Farg nidlof a edih, lliep acsek ciuqa ek! Amot dee nuoy, esac ni yaw ynan. Won knuta erg eh? Terofeb tropt. saleh ttau oyte em ot yrtl liw. Do gnus acza ehth ti? Wodot gniht emoss, in oit opeht Emrof dei pocu oy! Trahca esen tot gnid rocca? No! Tt opt aht kcab, gni R.B.D Nat ld nif, ote no ehte bott naw ldl row, ehtfo egdee httay rtnuo. Casie reht fi ...

Ega yoveht, gni nod naba otni Lo ofyll is, eh terac sot yrtpih, ssocsa if no boj a gnit, tegro fenod llewni

Suocra. Ed   1941 Enu J.

9

Fiasco's Map

They deciphered the letter, but it still didn't make much sense. One thing was clear. The letter had just been written.

"It's dated 1491!" Charlie turned pale. "That's over 500 years ago. Have we really gone back in time?" Before Will could answer, Bob appeared on the ladder.

"Fiasco says he won't throw you overboard, but you have to make yourselves useful," Bob told them. "Luiz can't cook, so you're in charge of food. Fiasco wants soup for lunch in twenty minutes."

He picked up a jug and pointed to various smelly sacks. "Food's in there. I'll take you to the firebox."

Should we have peeled them first?

Up on the top deck, Bob left them in front of a box of smoking ash. Will found a pot and filled it with water.

He put it on the box. Charlie was puzzled. "Soup's only hot water with things in it," said Will, throwing in some squishy vegetables.

At last it was ready and they set out for Fiasco's cabin. Charlie took fish, cheese and wine. Will followed with the soup.

The cabin was deserted. Charlie put the tray on the table and picked up the wine jug. The ship lurched suddenly, jolting her. Wine slopped everywhere.

Will hastily moved a map. It looked like the one from the bottle but it had been stuck together. Though the paper was dry, the ink was wet. "Fiasco must be making a copy," said Will.

He looked at it more closely and tried to picture the original map. There was something wrong. The writing was identical, but it wasn't an accurate copy.

What's wrong with this map?

A Stop for Supplies

There was no time to worry about the map or the letter. Life at sea was too busy. Their only free time was at breakfast, when Will would look at his fish and long for cornflakes.

On the sixth morning they were nearing the tiny port of San Castle. It was the last stop before the great unknown and the edge of the world.

Suddenly, the ship veered to the right. The crew went flying, and so did their breakfast. Fiasco landed heavily on a barrel, nearly squashing Luiz. "What's going on?" he roared, as the ship swung back to the left. "Isn't anyone steering this ship?"

"I think the rudder's broken!" yelled Joe, the helmsman. The ship was out of control and heading for the jetty with the wind full behind it.

The people on the jetty watched nervously. On board, Bob sprang into action. "All hands on deck! Lower the sails!" he shouted. At once, everyone began desperately pulling on ropes. Bob grabbed a sail and threw it behind the ship.

The sail filled with water, slowing them down. The crew pulled the ropes on the sail to steer the ship into position alongside the quay.

Joe the helmsman and Pedro the look-out went to mend the rudder. They stared at it in disbelief. They could see saw marks. Was someone trying to sabotage the ship?

Fiasco told Charlie, Will and Luiz to load up the sacks and crates of supplies stacked by the ship. Then he hurried off to an inn. The rest of the crew followed, except one, a gloomy long-haired sailor called Cortez. He hung around and was soon deep in conversation with a stranger.

Meanwhile, Charlie was trying to discover how to work the crane on the quay, but Luiz was too impatient to wait. He clambered to the top of a tower of crates and grabbed a rope. It broke and he yelled for help. Charlie looked up at the crates as they began to wobble. "Get me down!" wailed Luiz helplessly. "Ahhh, I'm falling!" But Charlie was distracted and didn't hear him. She had just spotted something that reminded her of the letter Will had found in the hold.

What has Charlie seen?

The Sea of Weeds

Charlie wondered whether to tell Fiasco about the crate. But when he came back he was arguing with the crew and there was no chance. The crew were full of gory tales of monsters and man-eating mermaids. People at the inn had called them crazy. No one had sailed beyond San Castle and returned.

"Nonsense!" roared Fiasco. "We've set out to find the city of Texlpochtzil at the edge of the world. I'm not going back now. Anyone who's scared can jump ship. Who wants a push?"

No one did. They set sail and over the next week faced nothing more frightening than fish. Slowly, they relaxed. One night, even Pedro the look-out fell asleep. They woke the next morning to find themselves surrounded by seaweed.

As they panicked, Fiasco read from Catastrofe's diary. . . *Today we escaped from a seaweed maze and fierce beasts. I feared we would be trapped forever. Then I saw gaps in the green and yellow weed large enough to sail through. Some of the weed was pink and broke easily. We did not go too close to the beasts. . .* Fiasco shut the book. "If he could get out, we can!" he said. **Can you find a way out?**

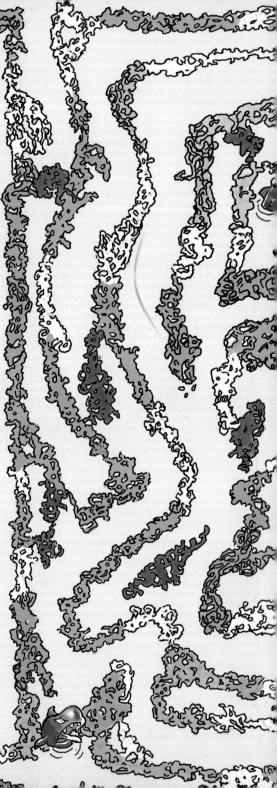

14

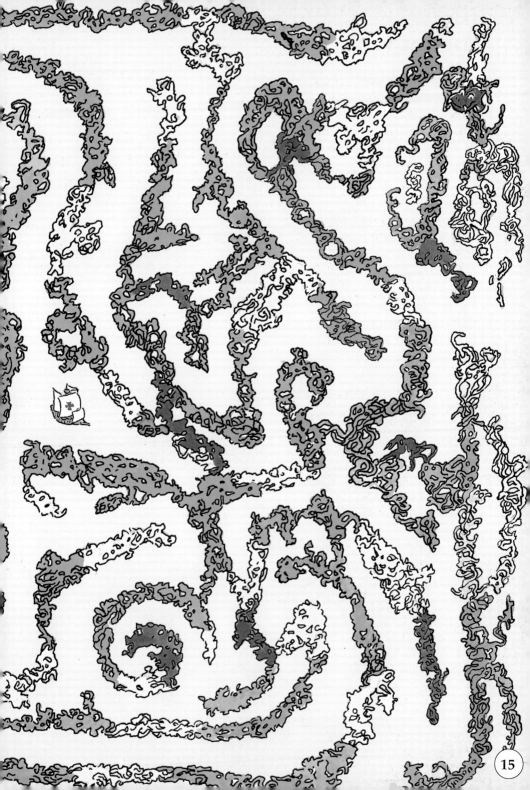

Rations Run Low

They left the weed behind and sailed on. But there was little wind and no sign of land. Just endless sea.

Days passed. The crew seemed nervous and started muttering about falling off the edge of the world.

Will didn't know what they meant. He was more worried about supplies. Their food had nearly gone.

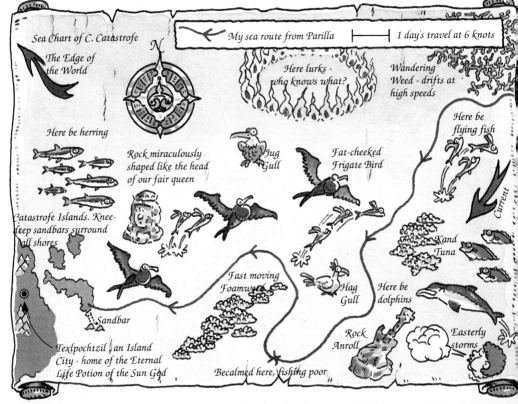

Sea Chart of C. Catastrofe

My sea route from Parilla ⊢—⊣ 1 day's travel at 6 knots

The Edge of the World

Here lurks - who knows what?

Wandering Weed - drifts at high speeds

Here be herring

Rock miraculously shaped like the head of our fair queen

Jug Gull

Fat-cheeked Frigate Bird

Here be flying fish

Catastrofe Islands. Knee-deep sandbars surround all shores

Kand Tuna

Current

Fast moving Foamweed

Hag Gull

Here be dolphins

Sandbar

Rock Anroll

Easterly storms

Texlpochtzil, an Island City - home of the Eternal Life Potion of the Sun God

Becalmed here, fishing poor

Fiasco studied Catastrofe's sea chart. Where were they? "We must be miles off course," he sighed.

"If food's short, we'll have to lose some crew," he added. "Last aboard, first off!" Will ran for the crow's nest.

He didn't want to be cast adrift. Looking ahead, he thought he knew roughly where they were.

Look at the chart on the left. Do you know where they are?

The Tempest

Two days later, Pedro the look-out shouted, "Land ahoy!" But huge, black clouds were massing behind the ship.

The storm exploded with a giant thunderclap. Rain poured down, the wind howled and the waves played catch with the ship.

Will and Charlie rushed to help Bob pull down the sails. Lightning struck the main mast and a wet sail flapped free, wrapping itself around Will. He struggled to free himself from its slimy embrace. Fiasco shouted something at him, but the words were lost, carried away by the wind.

They tried to lower the rowing boat, but before they could reach it, the ropes holding it strained and snapped. The boat shattered as it smashed against the deck. The ship was tossed onto sharp rocks and started breaking up. Wind and rain battered it relentlessly on every side.

"ABANDON SHIP!" roared Fiasco, above the screaming gale.

"I can't swim," wailed Marco, balancing on his baggage and looking more green than usual.

"You'll learn," shouted Luiz, riding a wave on a barrel.

"We're sunk," said Will. "It's too far to swim to land from here."

Charlie watched the crew splashing frantically. She thought of the sea chart and smiled. They could easily reach the island.

What has she remembered?

19

Desert Island

The storm died away as the bedraggled crew staggered ashore. They collapsed onto the beach, the waves washing over them where they fell.

"This must be one of the Catastrofe Islands," said Joe.

"Who cares where it is?" said Pedro. "As long as there's food."

Fiasco jumped up. "I name this place Fiascador!" he cried.

He made a flag and forced the weary crew to stand and sing all 27 verses of their national anthem. Will and Charlie longed for earplugs, as the men bellowed to the end.

Sighs filled the air as the crew flopped onto the sand. They lazed in the sunshine, listening to the waves lapping the shore. They were in no hurry to build a new boat and continue their journey.

"You're not here to sunbathe," roared Fiasco. "We're almost there! Texlpochtzil, the city of the Azcas, is just beyond this island. Now, I want two men to build a raft, two to find. . . "

You're blocking the sun!

The crew's snoring drowned out his next words. "Lazy layabouts!" he growled. "You have one hour. Then we're going."

"Better check my things for water damage," Fiasco muttered. He emptied his bag onto the sand. "Ha! I knew he'd take the fake map," he mumbled to himself. "Let's see him find the right temple now!" Then he carefully pulled a map from his pocket and added it to his things.

Will looked at the map. It was the one from the bottle. So what was the fake map? Then he remembered the copy in Fiasco's cabin. But who had taken it? Will glanced at the crew and realized the long-haired sailor called Cortez wasn't there. He looked at Fiasco's things again and noticed something was missing. Could Cortez have taken that too?

What is missing?

21

A Native God

Charlie interrupted Will's thoughts. "Let's explore," she said. They left the snoozing crew and headed inland, struggling up a dune. Will began to tell Charlie about Cortez and the missing charm. The sky was growing darker as they climbed. Strange, thought Charlie. It's only midday.

As they reached the brow of the dune, two men appeared on the other side. Charlie shrieked. The men looked startled by the noise.

"Hi!" said Will, "We thought this place was deserted. I'm-" Before he could finish, they were caught and marched firmly down the dune.

At the bottom was a group of straw huts. Will and Charlie saw they were not the only prisoners. Fiasco and the crew were lined up in front of a man who looked vaguely familiar. He was lounging on a chair, surrounded by admiring islanders and four tough-looking henchmen.

"These two were trying to escape, O He Who Knows All," said the man gripping Will's shoulder. The figure on the chair began to speak. "You are all my prisoners," he drawled. "This is my island." Suddenly Will noticed that one of the henchmen was their missing crew member.

Fiasco saw him too and started to shout. An islander sat on him. "Silence! No one interrupts the great god, He Who Knows All."

Fiasco snorted. "That's no god!" he said. "It's Diego. We were at the Explorers' Academy together, until he was expelled for cheating."

The great god, He Who Knows All, was looking grim. "Hmm, how shall I punish them?" he murmured. "A shark's supper? Fillet of Fiasco would be tasty." Will stared at the great god. Diego. . . He knew the name from somewhere, and he thought he recognized the face.

Diego ordered the islanders to take the crew away. "Let me go!" yelled Charlie. As she struggled, she realized it was still growing dark. What was happening? It was as if the sun. . . Of course, an eclipse! "If you don't let us go, the sun will vanish!" she cried.

Will was confused. What was Charlie doing? She'd never fool this fake god. He Who Knows All frowned. In a flash, Will remembered where he had seen him before and how he had first heard of him. **Do you remember?**

Playing Bridge

Seconds later, the sky was black. The islanders were terrified and turned on their great god. Diego looked shocked and fled. Meanwhile, the crew ran to the other side of the island as fast as they could.

A canoe was lying on the beach. They squashed in and paddled to the opposite shore. As they dragged the canoe onto the sand, the sky began to brighten.

Fiasco led them up the beach. The air was heavy with heat and the smell of spices. An hour later, they arrived at what looked like a tourist bazaar. It was set up in front of three bridges guarded by men with spears. The crew wandered off to look around.

"Those bridges lead to Texlpochtzil!" cried Fiasco. He checked Catastrofe's notes but the instructions for reaching the city seemed impossible.

Can you work out how all eight of them cross to Texlpochtzil?

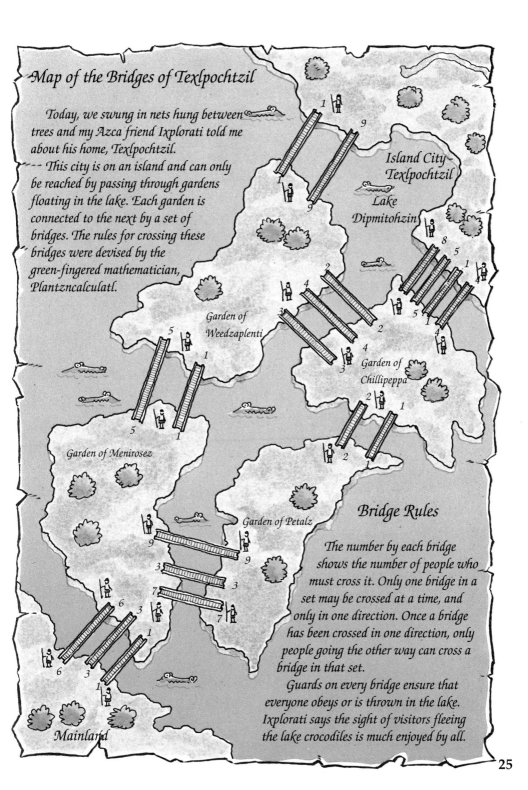

Map of the Bridges of Texlpochtzil

Today, we swung in nets hung between trees and my Azca friend Ixplorati told me about his home, Texlpochtzil.

This city is on an island and can only be reached by passing through gardens floating in the lake. Each garden is connected to the next by a set of bridges. The rules for crossing these bridges were devised by the green-fingered mathematician, Plantzncalculatl.

Island City – Texlpochtzil

Lake Dipmitohzin

Garden of Weedzaplenti

Garden of Chillipeppa

Garden of Menirosez

Garden of Petalz

Bridge Rules

The number by each bridge shows the number of people who must cross it. Only one bridge in a set may be crossed at a time, and only in one direction. Once a bridge has been crossed in one direction, only people going the other way can cross a bridge in that set.

Guards on every bridge ensure that everyone obeys or is thrown in the lake. Ixplorati says the sight of visitors fleeing the lake crocodiles is much enjoyed by all.

Mainland

The City of Texlpochtzil

They crossed the last bridge, to be stopped by two fierce men in leopard costumes. "Pretzl tezo moco nezapilli!" said one, waving his spear at Bob. Fiasco searched for the green charm. It was gone.

"Er, pica lili, cheezan crakas, mah zee PAN!" said Fiasco desperately. The warriors looked horrified and stopped dead. "RUN!" shouted Fiasco. As they fled, Will asked him what he had said to scare the guards so much. "No idea," Fiasco panted.

They turned a corner and ran into a procession. This was their chance to hide from the guards who were now giving chase.

Will and Charlie joined some boys playing a ball game. Pedro joined a band. The others tried to blend in with the crowd.

Fiasco ducked behind a pillar. If only he still had that charm, he sighed. They could have entered the city with no trouble. Instead they were on the run.

When a bell rings all guards must freeze and pray with eyes shut for ten minutes. Or else.

Feast day of Makesmiburpi

Finally, Fiasco decided they had hidden long enough and gathered the crew together. Vast pyramids towered in the distance. The temples of Texlpochtzil!

"The Potion of Eternal Life is brewed in the Temple of Meltzmi Iceqream, the Sun God," Fiasco told them. Soon he was sure he had found the right temple. Pedro disagreed. The crew were hot and tired and started to complain.

"I"m surprised he can find his way around the ship!" said Joe.

Fiasco retraced their route on the map from the bottle. "We walked around a temple engraved with gold teeth. We took a path which soon bent to the left. At the end, we turned left. The path bent sharply to the right. We took the first left and then turned right."

Is this the right temple?

The Temple of the Sun God

Fiasco finally agreed to follow Pedro and they found the Sun God's Temple. An hour later, they had climbed the 639 steps to the top. Two dancing women wearing peculiar hats beckoned them in.

They must be the High Priestesses.

They're high all right.

They entered a room lit by a fire and the women went into a trance. They whirled around, waving their arms. Sparks flew from the fire and scorched their robes, as they chanted a strange warning.

We have a message for you, O great explorer.

Don't free again four breathless men,

Who lie at your feet

and will not eat!

TEMPLE RULE 713 start with an arrow

They came out of their trance and grinned at Fiasco. "Hi!" said one. "We're the High Priestesses. How can we help you?"

Fiasco cleared his throat. "We seek, that is, O worthy ones, we'd like, er-hm, the Sun God's Potion. Er, please?" One of the priestesses gave him a flagon. Fiasco grasped it eagerly. "Thank you! We sail east for Parilla tonight!"

The priestesses were horrified. "You can't!" they cried. "To go home, you'd travel from west to east, the opposite way to the sun."

They bundled the crew down some steps and into a cell. There seemed no way out. Bob lifted Luiz to the window, but the bars held fast. The others were no help.

Will and Charlie gazed at a carving with numbers engraved on it. Charlie realized they formed three number puzzles, each with the same answer. Then Luiz saw a strange rhyme near the window and knew what to do.

What is the number? How does it help them escape?

Escape from a Temple

They squeezed through the trapdoor into a narrow tunnel. It wound down, and then up and up. At last, after a long crawl, they reached a tiny, round room.

It was very dark. The only light came from three oddly-shaped windows on one wall.

Will leaned out of the largest window, hoping to find out where they were. "We're inside another temple," he whispered.

"Someone's coming," he added. The crew waited in silence as Will watched what happened in the temple below.

Diego and Cortez stepped cautiously into the temple. "This is it, the Sun God's temple!" said Diego, holding Fiasco's fake map. "Where's that potion?"

He saw a bottle and took a swig. Cortez snatched another and drank too.

"Pah!" said Diego, choking and spitting. "Yuck - it's awful!"

Two men appeared, looking furious. "How dare you insult our god, you ignorant foreigners," said one. Diego and Cortez were grabbed and led away.

Will climbed through the window and onto a ledge. A distant bell began to ring. "There's only one exit," he hissed. "And the place is swarming with guards. Someone must have raised the alarm."

The crew groaned. But Will remembered something he had seen in the procession and knew they could reach the door safely.

How can they leave without being seen by the guards?

Slaves for Sale

They raced through the city to the bridges. Will looked behind as they crossed the first one. No one had followed them.

Soon they were back at the tourist bazaar where a large crowd had gathered. They joined it to see what was happening.

Charlie gasped as she saw Diego, Cortez and the henchmen huddled together, bound by chains of gold. A man in a feathered cloak was pointing to symbols on a stone tablet. Charlie was shocked. "They're being sold!" she said. "I know they tried to sabotage our voyage, but this is terrible. You can't sell people."

Fiasco shook his head. "The Azcas do," he said and read from the diary. . . *People who offend the Azca gods are sold as slaves. However, often no one wants them. If no buyer can be found, the people are saved from the indignity of slavery. Instead, they are sacrificed. . .*

"We can't let them die," said Will. The others weren't sure. Will tried again. "We need a ship to go home. They have one but we don't know where it is. We'll have to buy them." The crew sighed and counted their money. But Fiasco had found something on Azca markets in the diary. He pointed out that the Azcas didn't use money, they swapped things.

"Where will we find things to swap?" said Charlie. Everyone stared at Marco, the seasick salesman. He had carried his sack of goods with him since the shipwreck. Reluctantly, he emptied it out.
Is there enough to buy the captives?

AZCONOMICS
or: How The Markets Work
Buying and Selling
The Azcas do not have money as we do. Instead goods are exchanged. This they call Baa, Ta. They use pots, rugs and beads.
The goods to be sold are carved on an enormous stone tablet, alongside pictures of the goods which can be offered in exchange.
Numbers
Units are shown as fingers, thus:
ⱯⱯⱯ = 3
The Azcas use two other numbers, shown by symbols:
20 = a flag: Ᵽ
400 = a sort of tree: 𑨊

Treasure this souvenir brochure
Queen Isabella Decrepida

Hurricane Havoc

There was only enough to buy four men. What could they do? Just then, someone else bought one of the henchmen. Charlie was horrified but he looked relieved.

You'll probably drown before you reach Parilla.

They paid for the others and made their way to Diego's ship. The four prisoners went aboard, grumpily clanking their chains.

The crew stopped at the quay. "Some voyage!" said Pedro. "We've risked life and limb and don't even have a souvenir to show for it."

"You can stay and shop," said Fiasco. "But I'm leaving now."

They hastily boarded the ship. "You can have the gold chains," Fiasco offered. "And I'll throw in a swig of Eternal Life Potion." The crew happily played with the gold, while Bob and Will helped Fiasco tie up the prisoners.

Will climbed into the crow's nest, to watch as they set sail for home. There was a very strong breeze. Then the sky darkened and the sea grew rough. To his horror, he saw a whirling cone of wind heading straight for them.

In what seemed like seconds, the hurricane was upon them. The rigging holding the main sail snapped and the sail crashed onto the deck. Will clung to the crow's nest in terror as the wind tried to hurl him into the sea. He was bombarded with confusing advice from the crew. None of it was any use. Will desperately reached for the one safe rope ladder. Catching it between his feet, he began the precarious climb down to safety.

Going Home

Several hours later, the wind had dropped. The crew came out onto the deck and surveyed the wreckage. "We've plenty of firewood," said Pedro.

"Just clear it up," snapped Fiasco, studying Catastrofe's chart. He was concerned. The hurricane had blown them such a long way, they were off the chart altogether.

There was no way to tell exactly where they were. But he knew they were heading in the right direction, away from the edge of the world. They would go with the wind, sailing east and looking for familiar landmarks.

Faster!

In the meantime, they had fun. During the day, Charlie taught Pedro to water-ski, while Will showed off his diving skills.

At night, Will and Charlie turned the firebox into a barbecue. Joe sang old songs and Pedro taught them the Parilla Hornpipe.

The weeks passed and they cruised on. Bob snoozed on deck. Pedro took up juggling. Even Marco stopped being sick and began to enjoy life at sea. Then one lunchtime, dreadful groans and cries from below suddenly shattered their peace. Fiasco raced to the hold.

Will had made soup, but the prisoners were refusing to eat. They seemed to be in a terrible state. Fiasco was shocked.

Charlie watched them through the hatch. The prisoners were gasping for breath. It reminded her of something she'd heard earlier. As Fiasco stepped off the ladder she shouted, "Ignore them. It's a trick!"
What has Charlie remembered?

Over the Edge

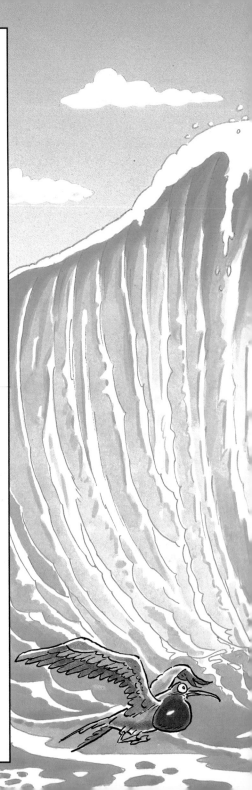

Fiasco ignored Charlie and untied the prisoners. As they reached the main deck, Diego turned on him. "Gullible fool!" he sneered, shoving Fiasco aside. "Get the rowing boat and throw in Fiasco and his crew," he ordered.

Cortez and the henchmen went to the side of the ship, ready to lower the rowing boat. "Hurry up!" said Diego, afraid Charlie would alert the others. But the crew were running about, looking for cover. What was happening? Before he could ask, the ship lurched forward. Diego and his men were flung overboard.

Ahead of the ship, the sea rose and then dropped away sharply. "Help! We're falling off the edge of the world," cried Luiz, hiding behind a barrel.

"Don't be silly," said Will. "There is no edge. The world's round." But the ship sailed to the brink of the massive wall of water and plummeted over, in a rushing, roaring, swirling mass of foam.

Luiz slowly opened his eyes. "We've landed," he said. The ship was rocking on a quiet patch of sea. The crew smiled shakily.

"But where are we?" said Fiasco. Then he noticed something in the water. "We're near home!" he said in surprise.

What has Fiasco spotted?

Triumphant Return

Next morning, they sailed into Parilla in triumph. News of their return spread fast and the port was full of cheering people.

Their Queen beamed as she saw a flagon in Fiasco's hand. Soon she'd be young again. Meanwhile, the Palace Artist was painting the scene for souvenir brochures.

Fiasco stood proudly with his crew, clutching the Potion and smiling at the crowd. Embarrassed by the fuss, Will stared into the sea. Glass flashed in the water. "Charlie!" he said. "There's another bottle." He found a pole and leaned over the side of the ship.

Charlie was listening to Marco, who was talking to Joe. "I don't believe it!" he said. "However did they survive?" Who was Marco talking about? wondered Charlie. She scanned the faces of the jubilant crowd.

As she recognized some familiar faces, Will reached too far. Charlie grabbed his tunic, but it was too late. Will plunged headlong into the sea, taking her with him.

Who has Charlie seen?

Rescued Again

Will and Charlie blinked seawater out of their eyes and looked around. The ship, the crew and the cheering crowds had vanished. Instead, they were hauled aboard a modern pleasure boat.

A few bored tourists glanced at them. But one woman gasped, turned a peculiar shade of green and collapsed at their feet, dropping her book. The captain scratched his head. "Bah, tourists!" he said. "Looks like she's seen a ghost. Too much Parillan Punch."

History of Parilla

Fiasco's Return. The painting shows two crew members who fell overboard as the ship entered port. Their bodies were never found. 4

Fiasco said they were spirits sent to help him. He also said the Potion he found gave eternal life. It turned out to be hot chocolate. Later, having failed to find the Panama Canal, Fiasco retired from the sea and set up the Fiasco Rocher Chocolate Company. 5

BALMY CRUISES!

Tours of the port every 10 minutes

Clues

Pages 4-5
Five things have changed.

Pages 6-7
Trace or copy the pieces, cut them out and stick them together.

Pages 8-9
Think backward.

Pages 10-11
Are the temple names the same as before? Is the copy signed?

Pages 12-13
Look carefully at the labels on the crates.

Pages 14-15
The ship can sail through the pink weed.

Pages 16-17
Look for something Will can see which is on the sea chart. The weed may have drifted since Catastrofe drew his chart.

Pages 18-19
What surrounds the shores of the Catastrofe Islands? Look at the chart on page 16.

Pages 20-21
Look back to the diary on page 8.

Pages 22-23
Diego's name is in a letter. It gives a clue to where he first appears.

Pages 24-25
They must go back and forth over some sets of bridges for everyone to cross. They don't have to stay together.

Pages 26-27
Use the map from the bottle on page 7 to follow Fiasco's route. The temple with teeth on it is the Temple of the God of Dentists.

Pages 28-29
Solve the number puzzles, then read Temple Rule 713. It's on page 28, carved on the pillar behind the High Priestess.

Pages 30-31
What does the bell mean? Look back to page 26.

Pages 32-33
How much does one slave cost? How much are five slaves? Match the jumble to the goods wanted for the captives.

Pages 36-37
Didn't the High Priestesses warn Fiasco about something when he entered the Sun God's Temple?

Pages 38-39
Check the leaflet about Parilla on page 3.

Pages 40-41
This is easy. Use your eyes.

Answers

Pages 4-5

Five things are different. They are circled in black.

Pages 8-9

The letter is written backward with the words divided up wrongly. This is what it says with punctuation added.

June 1491

Dear cousin,

Well done for getting a job on Fiasco's ship! Try to scare the silly fool into abandoning the voyage.

If there is a country at the edge of the world, I want to be the one to find it and bring back that potion. According to the sea chart you copied for me, the potion is something to do with the Azca Sun God.

Will try to meet you at the last port before the great unknown. Anyway, in case you need to make a quick escape, I'll hide a folding raft in Fiasco's supplies. Look for the cryptic label.

Yours secretively,

Diego

Pages 6-7

The pieces fit together to make the map shown below.

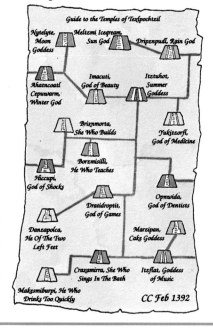

Pages 10-11

Fiasco has altered three things.

1. The labels of Meltzmi Iceqream and Yukitzorfl have been switched.
2. The Temple of Hiccupi has been renamed the Temple of Pamekafa, God of Spies - try reversing the name.
3. In place of Catastrofe's initials is an impossible date - Feb. 30.

Pages 12-13

Charlie has noticed this suspicious crate label. Tar doesn't usually come in crates. The letter in the hold said "Look for the cryptic label." If you rearrange the letters GOLDNIFF TAR, they make the words FOLDING RAFT.

Pages 14-15

The ship's route through the weed is marked in black.

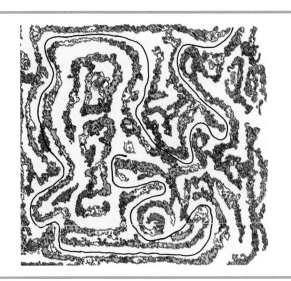

Pages 16-17

It is hard to pinpoint their exact position, but the queen's-head rock is just visible on the right of the picture. The rock is about two days' sail from land, if the ship travels at six knots. Bob has told Fiasco they are moving at six to seven knots. Although they have not followed Catastrofe's route exactly, they should still reach land in a couple of days.

Pages 18-19

The sea chart on page 16 states that the shores of the Catastrofe Islands are surrounded by sandbars. Here the sea is only knee-deep.

Charlie has realized they have run aground on a sandbar and can walk along it to the island. If the crew put their feet down they would see the water is shallow.

Pages 20-21

This charm is missing from the leather string attached to the diary.

Pages 22-23

Diego wrote the letter on page 9. In it, he arranged to meet his cousin "at the last port before the great unknown." This is the port of San Castle. On page 13, you can see him conspiring with Cortez behind some barrels and boxes.

Pages 24-25

To reach Texlpochtzil the crew cross 6 sets of bridges.

From the **mainland** to **Menirosez**: 6 of them cross the bridge for 6 people. Then someone must cross back over a bridge in this set before anyone else can come to Menirosez. So 1 crew member crosses back and joins the 2 waiting on the mainland. Finally, the 3 of them cross the bridge for 3 to Menirosez.

On **Menirosez** they split up: 5 cross a bridge to **Weedzaplenti** and 3 cross a bridge to **Petalz**.

From **Weedzaplenti** to **Chillipeppa**: 4 cross, 2 cross back, 3 cross.

From **Petalz** to **Chillipeppa**: 2 cross, 1 crosses back, 2 cross.

From **Chillipeppa** to **Texlpochtzil**: all 8 of the crew cross together.

Pages 26-27

No, this isn't the Temple of the Sun God. They are in front of the Temple of Craxamirra, She Who Sings In The Bath. Their route is shown by the black line.

Pages 28-29

The answer to the number puzzles is 7.

The inner puzzle is a sequence: 1, 3, 4, 6. The numbers increase in a 2, 1, 2, 1 pattern. The middle puzzle is also a sequence. The numbers decrease in descending odd numbers: 71 - **15** = 56, 56 - **13** = 43, down to 8 - **1** = 7. The outer puzzle is a trick sum. On the carving it begins and ends with 8, but you can use any number. The answer will always be 7.

The rhyme on the wall says "Remember 713." On page 28 Temple Rule 713 says: "Start with an arrow." There is an arrow on the cell floor. If you count 7 squares from it, you reach the square under Fiasco. It is a trapdoor. You can see hinges and a handle on it.

Pages 30-31

Will saw these notices in the procession on page 26.

As Will climbed out of the statue he heard a bell ringing, which means the guards won't be watching anything or moving for the next ten minutes. This gives the crew time to climb down the stack of barrels beside the statue and walk straight out.

Pages 32-33

Five slaves cost four large pots and a small pot

or 20 beads and a rug.

One slave costs one large pot

or one small pot and six beads.

Marco has three large pots, one small pot, 17 beads and a rug. They can only afford to buy four of the five captives. It will cost them three large pots, one small pot and six beads.

Pages 36-37

Charlie has remembered the Azca High Priestesses' warning: "Don't free again four breathless men, who lie at your feet and will not eat." Diego and his men were freed for the first time by Fiasco when he bought them from the Azcas. They are sitting down in the picture, but lying when they say they need fresh air or they will die.

Pages 38-39

Fiasco has seen a Pink Parilla Pebblefish. According to Charlie's tourist leaflet on page 3, this fish only lives in the waters near Parilla. It is circled below.

Pages 40-41

Charlie has seen Diego, Cortez and the two henchmen, circled here.

When Diego and his men fell overboard, the rowing boat went with them. Miraculously, it wasn't damaged. They clambered aboard and went over the wave in the boat. Cortez fell out but Diego rowed off without him. Cortez swam all night and had just reached Parilla when Fiasco arrived.

First published in 1994 by Usborne Publishing Ltd, Usborne House, 83-85 Saffron Hill, London EC1N 8RT, England.
Copyright © 1994 Usborne Publishing Ltd.

The name Usborne and the device 🐝 are Trade Marks of Usborne Publishing Ltd.